M. S. David

# The Orphaned Artist and the Mermaid's Eyes

A stroy and Painting BY
M. S. David

Copyright @2022 by (M. S. David)



This publication contains the opinions and ideas of its author. It is intended to provide helpful and informative material on the subjects addressed in the publication. The author and publisher specifically disclaim all responsibility for any liability, loss or risk, personal or otherwise, which is incurred as a consequence, directly or indirectly, of the use and application of any of the contents of this book.

WORKBOOK PRESS LLC
187 E Warm Springs Rd,
Suite B285, Las Vegas, NV 89119, USA

Website:        https://workbookpress.com/
Hotline:        1-888-818-4856
Email:          admin@workbookpress.com

Ordering Information:
Quantity sales. Special discounts are available on quantity purchases by corporations, associations, and others. For details, contact the publisher at the address above.

Library of Congress Control Number:
ISBN-13:        978-1-958176-20-7 (Paperback Version)
                978-1-958176-21-4 (Digital Version)

REV. DATE: 04/05/2022

# CONTENTS

Website: https://thebirdwithblueblood.com/

Facebook page:  The Bird with Blue Blood- Art Studio

# Acknowledgment

To the Family that treated Me as one of their own. "Sandy and Bayran" who embraced me for years, showed me all the support and care I needed and paved the way for my success with hope and creativity. You are a beacon in my memory, and I will never forget your love and support.

To my dear, wonderful, and beautiful teacher, Kaye, I extend my thanks and appreciation. I feel your support gave me the ability to be creative, and your tender heart and warm voice as you read beautiful storiesenriched my mind with words of hope and creativity.

# INTRODUCTION

## The Inspiration for my Writing and Paintings.

"The Orphaned and Artist Mermaid's Eyes"
When I was nine years old, a few days before my mother passed away. I visited her at the hospital. She was so weak at the time.      It was a moment I'll never forget. As I lay beside her, looking into her green eyes, I saw other colors reflecting in them. I saw Purple and bit of blue. Thus, I asked her, "What is your favorite color, Mum?" In a weak voice, she replied, "I like green, purple, and a bit of blue." I was about to tell her that I see the same colors she loves in her eyes. However, The doctor walked into the room at that moment. So, my dad pulled me away from my mother's arms. She liked the same colors I saw in her eyes. However, I never had a chance to talk to her again. The coincidence between my mother's love for the colors green purple and little blue with the same colors I saw in her eyes, inspired me to write this story.

# CHAPTER ONE

## A Moment of Happiness in a Painting

A vast sea, where the coast stretched around the horizon, its blue water mingling with the colour of the clear sky, like a mirror reflecting the light of a jewel in a princess's ring.

A cottage not far from the shore embraced a small family, where a child named Mark lived with his parents and elderly grandmother. The cottage and the sea and the sky formed beautiful scenery.

In the world of that three-year-old child, his happy life was as cheerful as Bing cherry trees in a beautiful garden. His young parents loved Mark so much, as he was the first and only child in his small family. His dad did all he could to make his little boy happy and grant him whatever he asked for. He taught his son how to draw and usually allowed him to join him in his studio. Mark loved to play with his father's colours.

Even his young mother chose to dress vividly just to bring joy to her beloved son. She loved him more than anything else; she took care of him and spent most of her time playing with him. She made him beautiful clothes with brilliant colours.

When The boy turned three, it was a special day in the child's life, filled with enjoyment and happiness. The family started the day by having a fabulous time sailing in their small boat. The sea was so calm, welcoming the beautiful, sunny day.

Many friends came from the town nearby to join the family, as no one wanted to miss such a pretty party near the beach. Everyone – the family and their friends – had dinner and fireworks on the beach near the sea and stayed until late at night.

By 10 p.m., the party was over, and the family returned home, while everyone else who'd been invited returned home as well, taking beautiful memories with them.

It was near midnight; the little boy was sleepy and wanted badly to go to his bed. However, the day was not finished yet. His dad still had one last thing planned – to create a painting for his wife and son.

***

The Mark's mother wore green, ready for the painting. Then she held the child between her arms against her beautiful green dress, and she followed her darling husband to his studio in one of the cottage's back rooms.

"I like the green on you, mum," said Mark.

"It is my favourite colour," she said. "*My green dress and your beautiful blue dress will be amazing in your dad's painting.*"

The boy smiled and hugged his mum tightly.

His dad set up the studio, ready to paint his lovely wife and his three-year-old child. Then he asked his beautiful, young wife to sit on a white rock that he'd fetched from the shore and placed in his studio.

Mark, in his blue dress, felt safe between his mum's arms, cuddling in the dreamy world, floating and filled with love. It was a special moment for a child of his age. He did not want to ever leave that warm lap. He looked to his father, who was mixing and placing the colours on the canvas using special brushes.

Then his dad looked at them with longing and said, "I want to put something from me in your painting as I cannot join you."

His lovely wife said, "You can use your woollen purple cloak as a background for our painting." It was her favourite piece that her husband wore, and he was seen dressed in it often, especially in the evenings.

Mark watched his dad take off his purple cloak and try to hang it as a background. He spread it behind Mark and his mum on the wall. At once, Mark stretched out his hand to catch his dad's cloak and embraced it, then used it to cover part of his body, showing his love for his father.

His dad came close to Mark and kissed him. Then he hugged him and his mother and said, "*I love you; I love you both so much. The two of you are the most precious thing in all my life!*"

His dad used his cloak as the background, and because Mark insisted on having something from his father in his hand, he handed him his purple handkerchief for the child to hold, instead of his cloak.

Mark's blue dress was visible against his mother's. The green, purple and a hint of blue were amazing colours that formed harmonious and charming hues. Mark became the focal point to his dad's painting through his shining blue dress.

*It was a fantastic, eternal moment that bonded three souls with honest love.*

The child kept moving his eyes toward his mother's face and then to his dad while he worked on their painting, until finally he peacefully closed his eyes and fell asleep. His innocent childhood made him imagine that the next day would be even better, and that he would continue his beautiful life forever.

However, what was coming was beyond the ability of a child his age to comprehend.

***

He woke, shocked, and heard a loud noise coming from downstairs. A voice shouting out horrible things that stole the happiness and peace from his life forever.

The same people the boy saw celebrating his birthday yesterday were gathered again that morning, but this time to witness the shift in his life.

His dad's boat was not where it was supposed to be. It had disappeared, and his parents were gone, forever leaving him alone, bare, facing his destiny with only his weak, elderly grandmother.

*The sea was so calm, as if filled with his emptiness.*

At once, the child shouted "Mum, Dad!" and then ran to his father's studio, hoping to see them. But instead, the child saw only his dad's painting still on the easel. It carried a more beautiful moment in the child's life than he would ever experience again.

*Mark stood in front of that painting, staring, lost in the darkness of the memories forever.*

# CHAPTER TWO

## The Orphaned Boy Grieving

The days passed slowly, with him feeling the loss of his lovely parents abandoning him in a world of loneliness and need. Yet, whenever the child's feet touched the sand of the shore, a flurry of thoughts drove him to that beautiful past.

His passion for his dad made him feel that his father's soul wandered in the studio and looked at him with love. But his dad's soul no longer had a place in his world. Thus, it caused only deep sadness whenever the boy came close to the cloak.

The orphaned boy was never seen playing near the sea as he had before; the studio became his special place to spend his time. He always remembered catching his dad's handkerchief to cover part of his body. The kiss that his dad had placed on his cheek before he fell asleep between his mum's arms resonated in himself and his mind. The studio continued giving him peace; *he enjoyed looking at his mum with her beautiful smile and green dress in his dad's painting.*

The boy did not want to leave that moment, wanting to be close to the painting of his mother.

***

Whenever Mark looked at the painting, he felt the warmth of his mother's arms. Tears dropped from his eyes as he talked silently to her, wanting his mum to come home. "Mum, I need you. Please come back." And then he ran to his grandma and begged her to search for her.

His young age meant he refused to comprehend that she was gone and was never coming back.

So instead, his grandma held him tight to her chest and told him, "Your Mum is the sunlight," and then she pointed to the small flower by the cottage door. "My dear, lovely, sweet boy…look over there. Do you see that sole blue flower on that plant?" His grandma referred to a blue rose by the cottage door. "That rose is like you."

"I am blue like a rose?" the boy said.

"And the sun like your mum," his grandma added. "My sweet boy, your mother will always be like the sunlight to the rose. Even though the flower can't see the sunlight, it still gets the power to live from the sun's presence. She will continue watching you from the seaside forever."

But the boy did not understand what his grandma was saying and continued to cry, begging his grandmother to search for his mum.

"Grandma, I want her to hold me and play with me again. I don't want her to be the sunlight. I just want her to come back."

The child left his grandmother to run to his dad's studio, holding his purple cloak. He sat on the white rock in front of the painting, viewing himself cuddling between his mother's arms. *The painting was glowing with green, purple and a little hint of blue.*

Days and months passed, and the boy never stopped sitting in front of that painting. No matter how much his grandmother tried to have him come back to his everyday life, still, the orphaned boy would not leave his memories.

Therefore, Grandma decided to move the painting to the boy's room, so he could see his mum's picture all the time.

But it wasn't the painting the boy was searching for. Instead, he was looking for his parents and anything to remind him of them. So, the boy never left the studio, and he was often found sleeping on the white rock where his mum had sat, in her green dress, for the last time.

His grandmother was very worried about him; thus, she decided to move the white rock and threw it away, hoping that might help the boy to forget. She called for help, and some friends from the town carried the white rock and threw it in the sea.

Mark watched them from his window, crying and begging them, "Grandma, no, please! I want it to be here."

His grandmother told him, "*My lovely boy, the white rock must go to the sea, where it belongs*. The sea is the place where your parents would have never stopped watching you."

The boy looked at the sea with hate because it had taken everything from him, even his memories. The boy did not want anything to remind him of the sea.

After that moment, he started to avoid the ocean and never went close to it. Even the coast, where he used to play on the sand, building castles, did not interest him anymore, as it was a part of the sea.

Even its blue colour, dominating the boy's small world, faded away.

*Instead, his dad's painting, and its hues of green, purple and just a hint of blue, lingered in his heart and mind.*

# CHAPTER THREE

## The Sea Fairy

S adness ruled the child's soul in relation to the memory of the warmth he'd lost that night, changing his life into a colourless palette. Loneliness haunted his soul with painful memories. Mark never left his dad's studio and spent a long time in front of his painting, making its colours resonate in his mind, leading him to imagine that everything in the world carried those colours.

However, his lonely existence made him easy prey for others to break into his life.

One day, Mark was sitting in front of the easel, looking at his dad's painting. As he was wrapped in his sadness, he felt that someone was watching him from behind the window. He turned his face but was only fast enough to catch the watcher's shadow.

He could imagine that shadow. It was that of a kid like him. Who was this child? What did he want from him?

All these questions hovered in his mind such that the orphan began to feel and think that it was all in his imagination.

So, he returned to his sadness, sitting silently while drops of tears started to wet his cheeks.

At that point, the shadow came back again, and this time he could see it. The shadow was a white, shiny-faced boy, who knocked on the window and started waving to him, asking him to follow his steps.

The boy was dressed in a green shirt, purple pants, and a blue hat.

The orphan walked towards the window, looking at the white boy smiling behind the glass.

"Come with me, let's play," the white boy said, and then ran towards the sea.

The orphan was surprised at seeing him dressed in green, purple and blue.

"Those colours are the same as in my dad's painting," he said to himself. He thought, *He must have been sent by my parents to be my friend.* The orphan ran to the main door, looking out at him.

However, he saw nobody there. All he could see on the sand was footsteps coloured with green, purple and a hint of blue. The boy had disappeared where the beach was, as usual, welcoming the sea's waves.

With the colours of the steps, he knew that the white boy wanted to provoke him to follow.

So, he followed the sand steps until he saw an uncompleted sketch on the sand, near the moving sea's waves. The orphan looked to the sketch of a horse, as if it was trying to move and fly.

The first thing that came to his mind was that the white boy had sketched the horse on the sand, but the horse was missing one leg, and it was not enough to make him able to move.

The orphan stretched his hand to touch its beautiful wings. The attractive colours that shaped the horse appeared in the same hues that the orphan loved.

The orphan was shocked, and he wanted to call his grandmother to see it. Instantly, he turned to go back to fetch his grandma. But instead, the horse called him by his name and said, *"Mark, please draw my other leg."*

***

One of the waves handed the orphan a stick, and with curiosity, he began to draw the horse's other leg on the sand.

Whenever the orphan made any mistakes, a sea wave pushed the sand to scratch it out. Immediately, when the boy was done with it, another big wave covered the entire sketch to drag it down to the bottom of the sea.

What returned was a lively, transparent horse made from water. Most of the horse's body was green with purple spots appearing all over, while its hair and tail were coloured with blue.

As soon as Mark saw the horse carrying those colours, he felt happy. The sea was attempting to lure the boy into being his friend again.

The horse came close to the amazed boy and took him to a beautiful new world, where the sea and its blue colour dominated the earth and the sky.

From that day, the white-faced child – a fairy – began calling the orphaned boy's name, inviting him to the sea. The orphan was the only one who could hear the voice.

# CHAPTER FOUR

## The Magic Journey

One day, Mark woke up, eager to see the sea more than ever before.

As he was making his way through the air that was coming off the ocean, the wind made his hair fly backward and his blue clothes cling to his slender body, while his steps diverged quickly to bring him closer to the shore.

As he reached the sands of the beach, they were saturated with water, but the sun's rays had drenched it with some warmth, making the sand seem dry, despite the rush of the waves.

The orphan, Mark extended his arms to the sea, and the sea once more handed him the stick carried by one of its waves. Then, quickly, the orphan began to draw on the sand – a ship piloted by seagulls, with enormous sails, many oars and large, bright-coloured shells in front of it.

He was so busy drawing that he did not raise his head to see anything around him. But after it was finished, the ship was a masterpiece of creativity and beauty in craftsmanship and splendour.

He moved backwards a little from the ship he had drawn to contemplate its beauty. It was so wonderful that even the sea waves did not help him erase the mistakes.

***

He was quite impressed with his drawing, so he looked at it and shouted, "I'm done; there's nothing left to add." Then he said, "Thank you, beautiful, bright, blue sea. *You have given me a great adventure by drawing this ship, which sent me to a world of imagination and creativity.*"

"How wonderful."

Immediately, the seawater rose gently, expressing the boy's happiness and joy. Then it threw one of its waves on the boy's drawing, which pulled the picture to its depths. After a moment of silence, the wave returned the sketch and transformed it into a real ship – a ship with seagulls, made of oak wood, and painted in a crystal-blue colour.

The boy said gently to the sea, "Could your waves send me to see the secrets of the world? I wish I could be the captain of a ship and get away from the shore."

The sea replied in the white boy's voice, "*You could travel and get away for as long you like. And you can come back whenever you want.*"

However, the sea continued talking with him, ignoring his question and encouraging him to climb onto the ship and play with its birds. Finally, the waves brought him to the ship's deck, and the ship's oars began moving on their own. It was all like magic.

A long time passed as the orphan boy sailed, having adventures on far away islands. He had blue wings, given to him by the sea, that allowed him to fly with the birds and discover the beauty of the sea and its colours.

Mark started to feel tired, so he returned to the beach, filled with wondrous stories. He looked proudly at his sketches on the sand and then ran to his grandmother, who'd been watching him from the cottage door while he had been busy playing and drawing. She felt so happy seeing him coming toward her as the reddish-purple sunset decorated the sky.

Mark entered the cottage, overjoyed after returning from his trip. He asked his grandmother for food and ate greedily.

Finally, he said, "Your food is delicious, Grandma."

His grandmother looked at him with a smile while busy with her own warm soup.

The orphan was so happy, enjoying being close to the sea again. *His imagination and the beauty of the sea had united to create a beautiful world, filled with adventures.*

# CHAPTER FIVE

## The Sea Creation

The grandmother sat contemplating the orphan and sighed because she had now become sure that there was nothing he would ever love more than the sea. She walked to one of the overlooking windows, sighing again while she gazed at the ocean. "I wish he had found a true friend to play with and save him from his loneliness, yet he seems to prefer the sea to everything," she said aloud to herself.

The sea listened to her and said back, *"I am his friend; I am his real inspiration."* Its wave started rising up and down, like a skilled dancer.

*"I created the white boy from my foam to share with him his innocent childhood, and it is time to show the orphaned boy my deed."*

On one of the bright, beautiful mornings while Mark was playing alone on the seashore, the waves appeared and gently touched his bare feet. Then, the sea began to send foamy waves to Mark in a magical flow. The rising foam, like white clouds falling over the water like pearls, reflected the sunlight. The sea created a scene as if it wanted the foam to attract the Mark 's eyes to something.

He greeted the ocean and stood looking at it. The white foam started to gather on the shore, getting closer to his feet and tempting him to touch it and enjoy its softness.

Mark loved the foam, he touched it with his hands, and it felt like he was playing with clouds. He kept feeling that fluctuating whiteness formed from seafoam until it started to fall from his fingers and returned to the sea again.

***

Meanwhile, a ball of pure white foam rolled towards him, and Mark picked it up with his hands, his palms filled with it. The foam was soft and fluffy, almost fading from its softness in Mark's hand.

Before it faded away completely, Mark threw it into the sea like a dove of peace and love. But before the foam ball fell into the coming waves, it disappeared. One of the waves stretched out to catch it, carrying the white foam to its depths.

It was quiet for a moment.

Then a boy appeared, as white as snow, taken by the waves to the shore where Mark stood – a boy made from seafoam.

It was transparent at first and then appeared as a boy the same age as Mark. The orphan was amazed and excited, looking joyfully at what seemed to be a new friend.

The seafoam boy was dressed in the colours Mark adored, wearing a green shirt, purple pants and a blue hat.

"I have seen him before," Mark murmured to himself, then asked him, "Are you the boy who used to call my name every morning?"

"Yes, I am the one who called your name each morning," the seafoam boy replied.

Excitedly, Mark said, "I would like to show you my drawings that I made on the sand!"

The seafoam boy jumped off the swaying wave, moving towards Mark.

"I saw them all before. I was here with you all the time. Only I was a form of water moving over your sketches. I was like a pair of hands, helping you refine your drawing." The seafoam boy moved his soft hands in the sand.

*"I knew there was someone who was with me all the time; that's why I never felt lonely."*

"I am part of the sea, a sea fairy. I was made to be your friend. I will always be with you," the seafoam boy said.

The boys walked and chatted, wandering between the varied and beautiful drawings that were spread over the sand.

Mark spoke to him in a cheerful voice, "I am so glad you are wearing those beautiful colours."

"Which colours?" the seafoam boy replied.

*"Green, purple and a hint of blue."*

The seafoam boy sounded offended as he said, *"Your eyes are deceiving you. You will see my real colours when your old memories leave your mind."*

The two boys became friends, playing and drawing together all day long. Then, at sunset, the seafoam boy walked Mark to his cottage.

Mark said, "Come in with me! My grandma must meet you."

With a few steps back, the seafoam boy said, "Well, unfortunately, no one except you can see me, and I have to go back to the sea, but don't worry, I will be here every morning to invite you to the world of the sea. I will always be here for a new adventure."

# CHAPTER SIX

## The Change

The seafoam boy was the ocean's endeavour to change the orphan's attitude and make him forget that it was the one who took his parents from his life, driven by jealousy to see anyone appreciate anything except it or its blue colour. The sea aimed to make Mark its artist, to show all the world its beauty after failing with his dad.

A few weeks later, the seafoam boy's clothes began to change gradually. The green, purple and blue faded away and switched to a shimmering blue, matching the colour of the sea.

Mark asked him, "Why did you change the colours of your *clothes*?"

"*I never changed. I am made from the sea.* So, the sea dressed me in gleaming blue clothes with sparkling silver beads of water that reflect its features and its hues. I am so happy you are starting to see my true colours."

Mark looked at him thoughtfully.

The seafoam smirked and stated, "*That means you've changed inside and have begun to love the sea and its blue colour.*"

The sea chanted loudly, "*No place for the green, purple and a hint of blue in your life anymore. Only the blue.*" The sea was proud of this change.

The ocean's colour attracted the child, and he started to feel that he belonged to its colour and serenity. The sea stretched out to touch the blue of the sky, like the best artist using his brushes to spread the colour across a canvas's surface, to create a spectrum of blue tones. It was like marvellous music.

# CHAPTER SEVEN

## The Artist of Maritime Paintings

The blue colour started to inspire the orphan and he derived beauty from it. Therefore, all his simple drawings in this colour began to express depth, beauty, serenity and hope.

He did not love or believe in anything, except in the colour of the ocean. He felt as if blue was music that spoke to him in harmonious tones, and that no other colour reflected in the sparkle of his honey eyes.

***

As Mark grew up, the sea became his subject and inspiration for painting, and Mark became one of the most famous artists in the city. He was well known among people as the painter of the sea. The sea was his purpose, the blue colour outshining all others in his paintings, and his art became a public spectacle.

He was the only one who knew the sea's language.

His ears learned to listen and understand the sea waves when they performed music. The waves entertained the artist by playing charming music on the rocks while he was painting, and the music gave his talent the light to bloom like lilies. The sound of the waves was like song, translating the beauty of nature.

The light summer wind stirring amidst the waves was his latest painting. It was a beautiful piece that showed the spirit of love and beauty. Purple was there in the painting, but only a little, just to show the sunset.

*"There is nothing in this world more worthy to be painted than the sea's beauty, and there is no colour more worthy of being used than blue,"* he said to himself.

Whenever the artist aspired to create a unique painting for the sea, the seafoam boy was there. They walked together on the soft sand or on the rocks.

The seafoam boy had never failed to help the artist, as he was one of the sea's fairies, made to drive the artist towards the world of blue, leading him, as usual, to the stunning spots where the artist could paint.

"Come with me," the seafoam boy said, "I would like to show you a new scene which you will never be able to deny." After a few steps, he resumed speaking, "Your new exhibition should embrace them, so the entire world will celebrate the sea's colour."

Without hesitation, the artist followed his best friend, sparked with his happiness and amazement, putting his whole being into every strike of the brushes that passed on his canvas, mixed with the colour blue.

# CHAPTER EIGHT

## Silence Before a New Passion

One night, the artist received happy news stating that the main art school in the city had accepted his work and wanted him to do an exhibition for the public in one of its main halls.

The sea shared this happy news with him, as it was alwayswatching. The sea proudly and arrogantly challenged the world of inspiration and all other colours, shouting out, *"The colour blue will be the only one in the  artist's life, and it must be the only source of his inspiration forever. The artist is mine. WhatI failed with his father, I achieved with his son."*

However, a deep, strong voice from nowhere echoed inside the sea, bringing fear and sadness and challenging the sea and its blue colour. "The fog tries to hide the object's world, but it can't linger in the air; as the wind sweeps it away, the truth will show again. Envy will not hide the truth; mixing purity with confusion will not be for long, as confusion will disappear away like the fog, and must show again through honesty."

***

Upon hearing the voice, the sea became ashamed of all the deeds that it had done in the past, making it tranquil and speechless, like an aged man sitting in the corner of an old, abandoned, dark place.

Mark was so happy about the news that he could not wait for the daylight. The artist went to the sea to share his happy news with it. He wanted its help to guide him. "I need your help, my real inspiration! They already consent to my ideas that the blue tones should be the only inspiration for all artists."

But the sea was silent, and the seafoam was absent in the dark. The orphaned artist shouted again with all his might, "My inspiration, the sea…it is time to guide me and show me the way to the amazing sceneries. It is time to show the world the beauty of blue!"

*Still, there was no response.*

***

And on that dark, overcast winter morning, something strange occurred – the loss of the sea's sounds. All those sounds that had been calling and welcoming him each morning had gone. The sea was tranquil, as if it was waiting for an enormous and strange storm to mix its pride with fear.

Surprisingly, Mark felt complete, even when he was ignored by his inspiration, the blue colour. It was as though a solid feeling invaded him, as if all the sea's majesty had transferred to him.

Mark was astonished and murmured, "*The sea might think it is the time to step aside, even for a little bit, so it can test my loyalty.*"

Mark realised this time that he needed to rely on his artist's senses to search for the best scene to draw.

"Even with this gloomy day, I must create a stunning painting. I must prove my love and loyalty to the sea. I will find the most beautiful place ever." The artist spoke with some sadness on his face because he was missing his friend. "I will find a gorgeous scene, and I will show it to my sea and to the entire world!"

With determination, Mark went looking for unique views for his canvas.

# CHAPTER NINE

## The White Rock and the Mermaid Eyes

The orphan artist sat down on a rock, overlooking the beauty of the

sea, resting from the long walk and carrying heavy thoughts. He repeatedly opened then closed his eyes, to give his creativity wings to fly in the unlimited space. He closed his eyes, placed his hands upon his eyelids, and started dreaming with a pure, free mind.

In his dream, Mark found something unexpected that had been gathering dust for a long time. He wanted to open his eyes again, but his soul feared waking up from the dream. He was swimming in his imagination like a tiny creature in the ocean, and he did not want to leave that world.

He took a deep breath and hoped his fantasy world, which was made from his inspiration and reality, would continue forever. However, it was a real subject, created by his gift and love, which surrounded him. He opened his eyes again to merge his dream with reality.

The ideal scene was the spirit of the fact, and it was just a dream, but unfortunately, he thought it was real. Mark could not believe what he saw. There was no doubt about it; this was a beauty with no equal.

***

He saw the same white rock that had been in his father's studio floating on the seawater, covered with foggy clouds. The uncertain shape emerged slowly, endeavouring to reach the artist's consciousness. It was like a mote of light emerging from the dark.

The fog started to fade away, leaving a beautiful girl who seemed like a mermaid sitting on the white rock and looking at him with a beautiful smile.

The waves stirred with enormous anger and calmed down again as if they had lost their last breath. And they stopped playing their rhythmical drum on the rocks while the world stared in amazement at what had happened.

The sea realised that it could not inspire the artist anymore, so it became silent and retreated with a smashed pride. The waves went away from the shore, taking their astonishment and disappointment on their heads.

An announcement was written in the wind: *"The moon can deceive and hide the truth only during the night and only when the sunshine reflects in other parts of the world. Yet when the sun shines, the truth tells that life reflects the sun's giving or blessing or open-handedness. So, the moon hides itself during the  sunshine. So, the sea hides as the true beauty appears."*

This was his new inspiration that had changed everything…

Extraordinary green eyes.

Only Mark could see the eyes' true colour; he could just catch the gleam of them. He was hardly able to bear the burden of their beauty. They were a pure green colour that embraced purple with a hint of blue. The blue was beating fast in her eyes, like a bird's heart.

Mark shouted, "She is a mermaid with beautiful green coloured eyes!"

# CHAPTER TEN

## The Artist's New Inspiration

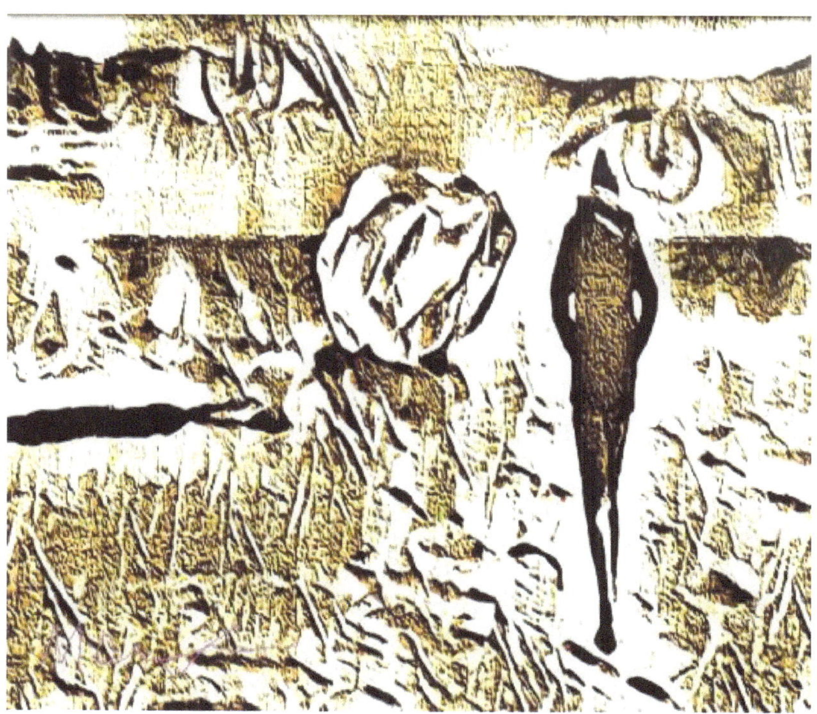

The Artist strolled to his new inspiration without watching his steps, carelessly bypassing the exposed rocks and stones that emerged from the sands.

However, the artist was shielded by the sea, which tried to save him. With determination, the sea sent one of its big waves, carrying soft, white sand from the sea bottom to disguise all the wild rocks that could hurt him, hoping Mark would defeat the repellent storm that hit him inside without notice, and come back to it again.

But Mark couldn't move his eyes from the mermaid's. *Something was dragging him to his old memories, as he saw green, purple and a  hint of blue in her eyes.*

Every part of his body was shaking with admiration, and his eyes stared into those spectacular orbs with unwavering awe and determination.

Mark could hear voices from everywhere, saying that her eyes were green. However, he was seeing something more than green in her eyes.

***

Then Mark gathered all his courage and asked, "What colour your eyes?" He wanted to be sure and hear it from her if the colour of her eyes was only green.

"Green! They are green and green only," she replied. He perceived the use of the word *only* as a hint at something else, as if she wanted to tell him that only he could see the true colours in her eyes.

"What? Green, only green?" Mark said the words slowly.

The sea, with all its might, shouted, "Yes! They are green and only green."

The owner of the eyes confirmed this.

Suddenly the seafoam boy – the sea fairy – appeared and spoke, "Come with me, leave this unwelcome visitor. Those colours cannot ever be your inspiration. They are not blue." He pointed to the sea.

But Mark could neither see him nor even hear his voice. Mark was not able to move his eyes from hers.

*Still, there was something dragging him to his old memories.*

The seafoam boy had not stopped trying to drive him to his old inspiration. However, Mark's mind was somewhere else, and he could not understand the sea's language anymore. Slowly, the seafoam boy faded away with his words.

Mark wondered, *Why do I see her eyes as green, surrounded with an aura of purple and a little bit of sparkling blue in the middle?*

Mark noticed that her big, beautiful eyes reflected the colours of the things around her. Wherever she turned her eyes, their colours changed.

Mark murmured, "I am reflected in her eyes as green, purple and a little hint blue! That why I am the only one who can see those colours in her eyes."

The artist leaned his head down and thought, *But I dress in blue; her eyes should have reflected the blue whenever she looked at me. So why do I see green, purple and a hint of blue in her eyes? Am I seeing my true self in her eyes?*

He remembered his dad's painting and that lovely moment resting in his mother's arms. But unfortunately, that painting had been missing, along with his grandmother, since the sea waves had visited his cottage a long time ago, leaving debris behind.

"Have I been blinded and deceived by what I thought for a long time was my true inspiration…the blue, the sea?" Mark murmured. "Have I just been set free from a great prison?"

# CHAPTER ELEVEN

## The Artist's Secret

The authentic colours of her green eyes had stolen the artist's sight. He became blind to see any other colour but the colours of her eyes.

*But what beautiful colour!* he thought silently.

She smiled and spoke with deep passion, as if reading his mind, "I love green, purple and a little hint of blue."

Mark paused for a while and repeated, "You love those colours?" His mouth opened in shock. *"She loves the same colours that I see in her eyes. I am those colours in her eyes. She must love me."* He concluded.

He decided that was his secret which he would keep to himself and never tell her about.

"That must be my genuine inspiration," he said. "I will paint the owner of the green eyes! Yes! I must have green, purple and a little hint of blue in all my paintings."

Mark glowed with happiness when she consented to him painting her. So, he ran back to his easel and his colours' bag, but then he remembered that he had no green, for all his colours were dominated by blue.

"I will throw them all away. I do not need to have this colour in my palette again," he declared, speaking of the blue paint. Then he paused for a minute and considered, "Maybe I will keep just a little, the same amount that is in her eyes."

Mark got all the oil colours out of his bag and threw them in the sea, one by one. However, he kept a small tube with a little blue. As the artist relinquished the colours into the sea, light and happiness grew in his heart like the spread of the morning on the green meadows.

***

With sadness, the waves took in the oil colours, mixing them with their blue. They blended softly in the water, like the vanishing snows on the mountains during spring.

The sea's frustration made the sea level fall away from the shoreline, fading its influence on the artist's creativity.

However, the little bit of blue which Mark had kept in his bag gave the sea a little hope. *One day, the blue colour might be gleaming again in the artist's life.* Thus, his old inspiration endeavoured to watch him from a distance.

Mark went back to looking at his new inspiration. Immediately, the fabulous inspiration granted him a new colours bag.

"Take this bag; you will find all the colours you need," the mermaid with green eyes said.

Mark was so happy as he held a palette cumulated with green, purple and a little hint of blue. At once, his entire world changed to hold just those colours.

# CHAPTER TWELVE

## Imploring the Sun to Stay

So, Mark started painting his new inspiration. He was amazed by her beauty.

"Here and there," Mark said, finalising the painting by placing green first and then the aura of purple and a little a hint of blue in the eyes' irises.

"I am done!" he shouted. Or so he thought.

"But something is missing," a sound conversed with him from within his painting. "Her eyes are craving for something, and you must find out what before the sunset."

The voice was echoed in his heart with each heartbeat. *Hasten, hasten! The time will pass swiftly.*

"I know that!" he murmured to himself, while looking to the sun. "Help me," he begged the sun. "I did everything as I was supposed to. I embedded the green, the purple and the little hint of blue beautifully in her eyes."

***

Mark stared at the painting, trying desperately to solve the mystery. He wanted to show her the artwork before the sunset.

"Quickly, you do not have time," the voice coming from his painting continued to surround him like a dark shadow.

Mark ventured to ignore the voice, and immediately he directed the canvas towards the mermaid, who was still sitting on the white rock with a fabulous smile.

She closed her eyes, and the fog started covering his inspiration. Then he heard a voice coming from the fog, saying, "*Listen well…your colours are still far away from resembling the truth of her eyes. The green, purple and little hint of blue are still without meaning and life, as if they are matching the shadows of death.*"

"Please wait! Give me a chance to correct my mistake. There is still time before the sun sets!" he screamed with fear. "Sorry for my stupid mistake. I promise I will never show it again if it is not complete."

The fog moved away from his inspiration, willing to give him another moment to do his painting, and her eyes opened again.

However, the time never stopped ticking away; the sun began to descend into the dark.

The darkness's hands immediately stretched between the artist and his inspiration, until her features were hidden. And his painting was covered by night, like eyelids embracing sleep.

Mark screamed, imploring the sun to stay. "Please, do not go! Her eyes will be directed somewhere else, away from mine. I can't bear to be apart from them. Do not give the dark a reason to take away the most amazing and beautiful thing I have ever seen!"

His easel shook under his brushes with each point or line he painted.

But the sun did not listen to him.

The last rays wrote words on the horizon before it was gone: *It is my duty to leave this world, as there are many souls dependant on my light and warmth. They have been waiting. The night was long, cold and painful for them. I must give them the warmth needed and hug them with the truth. My light will lead them to the right path and shield them from loss. They are waiting. I have to go now, but I will come tomorrow with new hope. That is my promise."*

However, the artist couldn't bear to see his inspiration fading slowly in front of his eyes. "Do not go…please," he repeated many times.

But the sun's rays started to disappear one after another, and things that had been filled with vivid colours started to hide in the darkness of the night.

Mark never stopped urging the sun to give him some of its light to finish his painting. He was terrified that he would lose his new inspiration forever.

His eyes and mind were both closed from seeing or thinking about anything except her, and the last thing that he saw was her eyes, as the final ray of sun reached them.

As time descended towards the night, second after second, his hope faded away, leading to a weakening of his breathing and his heart losing the desire to continue its beating.

The sea screamed with passion, wanting him to wake up. The waves knocked the rocks with anger. Yet Mark was still unconsciously roaming and reeling.

Suddenly, the sea commanded its waves to slide between the rocks, to wash away the layers of sand covering them. And it carried the sand to where it belonged, to the bottom of the sea, leaving the stones bare under the artist's feet. The ocean wanted to shock him with some pain, so that it might wake him up again.

It was not long until Mark 's knees bled as he fell on the naked rocks.

# CHAPTER THIRTEEN

## The Night Destroys His Hope

Mark gathered himself again and spoke to the sun, his words reverberating around him. "Please, please do not go. All I need is one ray to stay."

Mark still believed that the last ray could stay with him, even though, as time passed, the beam became more vulnerable to the dark.

The last glare of the sun continued lighting her eyes and part of his canvas while Mark tried to mix his colours, hoping that she would be content with his painting.

The dilemma was still living within him. He still did not know how to improve the colour of the mermaid's eyes on his canvas. Mark looked at his painting one last time and then to the sunray, worrying that the ray would leave him.

The sun was silent, understanding that the artist would never figure out what was missing in his painting, as he was still unprepared and needed time to grow in his experience.

The sun started to disappear from the world.

*"I beg you to permit only this last ray of your light to stay and brighten my mermaid's eyes."*

The last glare of the sun stretched again, and the last ray became stronger, fighting the dark, as if the sun agreed to give him more time to complete his painting.

***

But the night was so dark, and it had never let anything defeat it, even to relinquish a little place in its darkened world. The dark was like a monster following the rays of the sun, dominating and swallowing them one by one.

The last ray tried hard to stay and act like a lantern, helping the artist with his dilemma. Finally, however, the night squeezed the thin ray's thread between its arms and broke it to pieces.

The ray changed into drops of water as if they were the sun's tears, showing it was sorry.

The night left Mark hopelessly facing his destiny, giving a broad smile and wrapping everything in its dark cloak, declaring its kingdom. And it brought with it a dark cloud along with the severe cold, featuring profoundly in its darkness.

# CHAPTER FOURTEEN

## The Night Speaks

The night had taken reality from him, but it could not take away his dream.

Mark sat on the rough rocks, bowing his head in his hands. Tears flooded his cheeks and his loud scream roamed through the dark.

"Boy, why do you cry?" a voice called to him. It was coming from everywhere, from all sides around him. It was rising from one side and lowering on the other, like an invisible person moving in circles around the artist.

Mark stopped crying and then turned his face, trying hopelessly to follow the sound source. "Who is that?" Mark asked.

"I am the night."

"You are? The darkness that, with its arrival, took my soul away? Why did you take my inspiration away from me? The mermaid was sitting there, shining with her green dress and green eyes, just before you came."

"What, me? Take your inspiration? Why should I do that? I am just obeying the law of creation. *I am here to give peace and rest to all souls that have had a long, unrestful day! I am the one who gives beautiful dreams to poor and starving people, taking them to worlds that they have never been before and giving them wings to fly away from their brutal and ungracious day," the night replied proudly.*

"But you have made me become lost in the darkness when I had just found myself. You have taken all that I thought for a moment had become mine. Why did you not give me a little time? Why did you massacre even the last bit of hope that I had? Only one ray of the sun was all I wanted." Mark stood and murmured, "She loves green and purple and a little hint of a blue…the same colours I saw in her eyes."

"Wait, boy, listen," spoke the night. "People ask eagerly to have the things they love; they fall in the trap of ignoring things that might bestow them the wisdom to reach their perfection."

Mark roamed away from the invisible voice's owner, revealing his unwillingness to listen to the night.

Hours passed in the long winter night. Mark was watched by the night, trying to be his friend.

Mark walked with carelessness through the dark with bare feet, and so many times was about to stumble on the rocks laying everywhere on the beach.

"Be careful, boy! You will hurt yourself." The night showed its kindness to the artist, and as a result pushed all the winter's clouds away, letting the moon shine and the stars fill the sky.

Mark thought the moonlight might help him see her. So, he went to complete his painting, however he discovered it was lost, and he could not find his painting.

The night did not want to help him with his purpose, so it hid his painting. The night's goal was to entertain the artist and teach him that he could find beauty and inspiration with the presence of the darkness.

"Look to the stars; do you see the beauty of them? I am, myself, a great inspiration and bestow it to whoever wants it," the night whispered in the artist's ears, wishing to lure him in so that he would neglect his beloved inspiration.

***

Mark sat on the beach, staring at one of his hands which was filled with yellowish sand that almost looked like gold dust. The gold sand reflected in the moonlight.

The night became proud, showing what it thought was real inspiration that would distract and change the artist's mind.

# CHAPTER FIFTEEN

# The Truth of Green, Purple, and a Hint of Blue

Whenever Mark turned his face, he saw the night stretch its dark hands to blind his eyes, with the exception of the things the night allowed the artist to see.

"Look over there! In the sky, the blue shows within the beauty of the stars. They are shimmering with a transparent blue tone on the surface of the water," said the night. "Boy, do you not think the sea deserves to be praised when it allows the stars to reflect on its surface, like gorgeous girls looking in the mirror?"

The sea became filled with happiness when it heard the night mention its name. They shared the same desire to bring the artist back to his old inspiration: the blue colour.

Still, Mark was straying, his mind far away, repeating what she had told him, *that she loved green, purple and a hint of blue.*

However, everyone was shocked to hear him say, "She loved me. Her eyes reflected me, and I am those colours in her eyes. I am the green, purple and a hint of blue in her eyes. She did not know, she did not know," he repeated again and again.

Everything had changed. As each minute passed, Mark made the sea feel disappointment, as he was moving further away from his old inspiration, the blue colour.

"Why can't I see the blue colour again? All I can see is a little bit of it swimming in the ocean of green, surrounded with an aura of purple." He still saw her green eyes, shaded with purple and a little hint of blue in them.

Mark spent all the night talking to himself, unrestful, sad, and sorrowful.

# CHAPTER SIXTEEN

## The Night Leaves

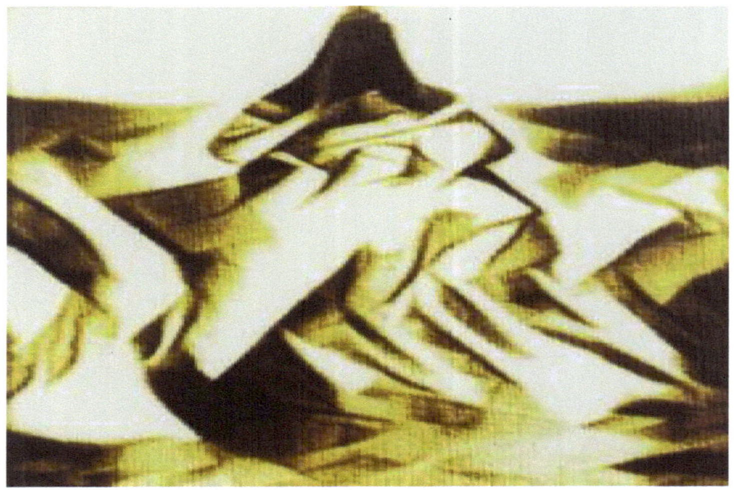

Gazing at the sky, which was full of incredible stars, it was impossible to be seen at this time of year.

"Where are your blue colours? Why do you appear green at this time of night?" he questioned the stars. "You and I have been overtaken by the words of the owner of the green eyes." That was what the artist had concluded.

"We are blue, only blue," chirped the stars like birds in heaven. The stars were like notes of music scattered everywhere in the sky.

Some appeared, and others disappeared, but the stars could not help comforting the artist.

The sea and the night were listening to him, and they recognised the sad fact that blue was not inspiring the artist anymore, because the stars were still dressed in the same blue colours, and they had not changed, as the artist believed they had.

The night's soul was surprised to see the morning star trying to shine so early.

"It is not your time to appear. It would be best if you waited; we are still hours away from the middle of the night. I am still ruling the world here," the night claimed. When it heard no reply, the darkness screamed, "Go away! You are not welcome at this time!"

The morning resisted what he said and pushed the dark's hands away. "You must leave. Do you not see what you have done?" the morning star said.

"I still have time, and I will make the artist return back to his real inspiration, the colour blue," the darkness said with anger.

The morning star interrupted the night, "Look at his face and listen to his words; your darkness will never be able to hide the truth anymore."

The night observed the pain and sadness coming out of the artist's face like a flood and realised that even its deep darkness was powered by the artist's pain. The night felt shame and decided to leave early, taking with it all the gloomy clouds.

At once, the morning star announced a new enjoyable day, filled with bright sunlight. The sun was given the power to rule the kingdom of life again.

Pleasure and hope passed across Mark 's face, but he became worried when he saw the morning star, as he saw it as a sign of the end of the night, and he wondered if he would see her again.

"Am I going to see her again? Or did the sea take her away?" Mark asked himself. "The sea took everything from me."

*The sea was listening with shame, as it was the one who took his parents, his grandmother, the white rock, and his dad's painting.*

***

Mark felt a heavy burden, resembling a mountain's weight leaning on his shoulder. Yesterday, he had not wanted the last ray of light to depart his world because he feared losing his new inspiration. However, today, more than ever before, he was worried that the first ray of the sunlight would not reveal her eyes.

Yet, his worry mixed with a tentative hope. He reassured himself that he would see her again, but an evil voice was growing from inside him, saying, "No, you won't; she is gone."

Mark shouted firmly, *"I will see her again! I will put everything: my soul, emotions and thoughts into that painting."*

The sun started to shine again, surrounding the world with warm lights. Birds and creatures greeted the sun with welcoming songs and spectacular smiles. The sun's rays were like crystals moving on the water's surface. The blue colour dominated the sea and the sky, as before.

He was so excited to see her again. Mark spent the whole day roaming around looking, searching, and hoping to see her again. Everywhere he walked, he shouted, "The green-eyed girl! The green-eyed girl!"

But she had disappeared forever. She had gone and taken all the splendid things with her. And the artist's world was now a dark stone, devoid of life.

But, nevertheless, he still had a little hope. Mark told himself, *she will breeze in again; I should wait for her.*

Mark shouted with all his might, "My mermaid, the green-eyed girl!"

But there was no response.

# CHAPTER SEVENTEEN

## The Sea Steps Away

Mark 's old inspiration, the sea, was burning from anger such that the seabed turned into erupting volcanoes. The sea was shocked to see the artist becoming a statue, standing there, lonely, without any movement. Mark wished with all his might to see again what he thought was a beautiful mermaid.

The blue colour, at last, had decided to step aside, accepting the new reality that other colours inspired the artist more than blue.

The sea tried to show its passion by playing its music again, but this time with sad tones. The rocks were shaking like drums, and the waves were like the most skilled drummers that had been ever heard. The wind blew hard through the wrecked ships to add a new melody to the sea's music. It played everywhere along the beach. All kinds of birds were spread, hovering with their wings to perform sad melodies.

*The sea tried to tell him, "I am your inspiration. Come back to me. We cannot be apart from each other."*

However, the artist's facial features showed that he did not understand the sea's language as before. His language now consisted of little words repeated in her sweet voice, "*Green with purple and a little hint of blue.*" That was what she had told him when he had asked her what colours she liked.

She had thought that her eyes were only green. And that was his secret, because he did not tell her that her eyes carried the same colours she loved.

***

Suddenly, Mark was startled, his mind and soul listening to the melody of her music which was singing to him. She loved green colours with purple and a little hint of blue. Mark's soul was hovering in the world of inspiration. Her eyes were shimmering in front of him with green, purple and a little hint of blue in them.

Then, the shape of a child emerged from the sea and came close to him. "Do you remember me?" the seafoam boy asked.

Mark was weak, his head bent down, but his head raised when he heard the voice. "You! My old friend! What amazing colours that you are dressed in this time! Green, purple and a hint of blue. It is like it was only yesterday when you knocked on the window and invited me to play on the seashore."

At once, the boy faded away to a pile of seafoam on the beach, as the artist had failed to see him in his real blue colour.

# CHAPTER EIGHTEEN

## Spring and the World of Inspiration

At that moment, a female voice spoke slowly but thoughtfully, "Boy."

Mark looked around him, rummaging for the owner's voice: "Who is that? Who is trying to talk to me?" Mark asked, looking around him.

"Me, the white rock. Look in front of you. I am floating on the mist just above the seawater."

Mark's facial expression glowed with happiness at once, and he cried, "A green-eyed girl, my inspiration! Where are you? I have been waiting here for you. I have never turned my heart away from you, even for a second."

Mark knew it was the same white rock that the green-eyed girl had been sitting on that magical day when she shone in front of him with her beautiful smile. Mark thought he would see her sitting on the white rock again, but, instead, when the fog faded away, the white rock stood there by itself.

The rock spoke again, "You must go to spring!'"

"Spring?" Mark replied.

"*Yes, you will know the secret and you will grow in your experience!*" The voice stopped for a minute and then spoke again, "*You may meet what you are looking for.*"

"Do you mean I will see her?" Mark urged, eager to know.

***

The white rock spoke again, "She represented the truth inside you; go to spring. Spring has all kinds of beautiful green colours. It glows with blooming trees, purple flowers and a little blue in the butterflies. *She will meet you in spring, so go to spring. Go! And ask about her!*"

"Spring, spring!" Mark repeated the word, and then he looked to the clouds. "Spring is still far away. How can I go there when we are still living in winter?" His eyes filled with sadness as he could no longer endure being away from her.

Immediately, the white rock turned into tiny pieces of white dust, hovering in the air over the sea, near the beach. And then the spiral of dust moved slowly towards the artist.

The sea was watching with eyes of revenge, and it sent one of its waves to hit groups of rocks on the beach, so that it might destroy the dust. Instead, however, a sprinkle of water spread out in the air and penetrated through the white rock's dust. So instead of washing the dust away through the waves' water, each tiny dust spec held a grain of water and continued spiralling in the air.

Then the dust, carrying the water's grains, came to surround the artist with a small but spectacular tornado and started to circle him. Then, suddenly, a breeze of wind pushed the cloud away to give the sunlight space to shine through each dot of water held by the white dust.

It created a great mixture of colours that turned into countless amazing rainbows in all tones of green, purple and a hint of blue.

***

The Artist was amazed. He concentrated on that scene, seeing only the colours that resembled what the green-eyed girl loved.

Slowly, the circles of colours gathered to turn into a mirror, surrounding and reflecting him. Mark saw himself as a bluebird, surrounded by mist. Eventually, Mark himself withered away and started living within that bluebird.

Thick fog, like a white cloth, limited the bird's – Mark's – sight from recognising anything around him. The bluebird felt as if he was standing on what he guessed to be a broken branch of a naked tree. Yet he did not care, as her song still gave him hope – green, purple and a little blue – and that was what she had told him she loved.

# CHAPTER NINETEEN

## His Mother's Eyes Were Green

"Go, search for your inspiration. Ultimately, you might find what you are looking for, the green, purple and a hint of blue, and then you can give perfection to your painting. Hopefully, that will bring peace to your soul again," the fog said.

Mark replied, "Yes, I will do anything so that we can meet again."

Finally, the fog started to disappear in front of him, and he could see the stunning sight of spring and smell the beautiful flowers.

It was spring here, and he hoped he would find what he was looking for: real beauty, real inspiration and all the beautiful colours.

He saw the magical purple sky with all its different tones and the purple flowers. The blue existed in the vast fields like shiny dots; it was in the roses or the butterflies' wings. Birds with all kinds of colours filled the sky and the trees.

The spring said, "*I will be your subject and your inspiration forever.*"

Mark was very excited to hear that and started looking around. Green erupted and the purple flowers with a hint of blue appeared. But there was nothing that could match her beauty.

Mark 's canvas was still without any colours, and time stopped moving again. Everything became silent. The spring listened to his voice, which was shaking with deep sadness, repeating what she had told him, that she loved green, purple and a hint of blue.

Mark 's sad feelings made the spring lose its brightness; thus, all the trees' leaves and flowers fell, and the gloomy winter came again.

***

He continued wandering without purpose or hope until he was stood in front of a black river, which reflected the dark, cloudy sky. Mark looked at himself in the water with a sad expression on his face. He understood now what the painting missed, as he saw the water not reflecting his image, *but instead reflecting his father's last painting.*

Everything was clear to him now. As he glanced at the water, he was looking at those last beautiful moments which he had shared with his mum and dad in the studio.

*"I am what was missing in my painting,"* he said, and remembered his mum's image. She was looking at him with her green eyes and beautiful smile, and he started to cry. It was the first time Mark had ignored the mention of the mermaid's name, the green-eyed girl.

Tears dropped, one after one, from his eyes and into the water. The river took the tears from his cheek even before they fell in it. Then suddenly, the river stirred, mixing the water with his tears, and forming a boat from them.

A few words were written on the ship in a strange and mysterious language: *Your destiny will start here, from the moment you get in.*

Mark stepped into the boat, and it sailed him down the river to the sea again. He came face to face with his painting, which was still in the same place on his easel, waiting for him.

It was an amazing painting that showed a woman sitting on the white rock with her green dress and looking at him with her beautiful smile. *However, she was not the mermaid.*

# CHAPTER TWENTY

## The Artist and His Painting Become One

The painting portrayed the same colours as his dad's last painting. Green, purple and a hint of blue were the main colours.

The orphan could see it clearly now. He had always thought that painting was for the mermaid. *But, instead, it was for his mum.*

Seeing the white rock had led him back to his childhood, when he and his mum had been the subjects of his dad's last painting. His passion for that missing moment had led him to paint his mum with her green dress holding a blue handkerchief in one of her hands. Mark saw himself as the blue handkerchief in his painting.

It was a fantastic moment that had lived in his inner feelings forever.

He remembered when he had stared into his mum's green eyes. They had reflected green, purple and a hint of blue. And just before he had fallen asleep peacefully between her arms, he had asked her what colours she liked. *She was the one who had told him that she liked green, purple and a hint of blue.* He had eagerly wanted to let her know that he saw the same colours in her eyes, but unfortunately, the boy fell asleep before he did.

All he needed was a little motivation to bring him to that childhood memory, and the trigger was the white rock.

*"She was not a mermaid as I thought. It was my mum's painting. I painted my mum."*

He realised that the colours – green, purple and a hint of blue – weren't enough to harmonise the colours of her eyes because her eyes were reflecting the inner him.

"The beauty of her eyes would never reach perfection without me," he said to himself. Mark felt that he could not live without living in those moments.

*"My soul would be the life in my mum's eyes, shown through the vivid colours. The painting was missing me. I cannot bear to live anymore. I must go; my world should be that moment, and I must be united with it."*

Mark began to cry as he thought of his mum and dad.

Mark stood without movement and with a broken heart, turning his eyes towards the sea. But, as usual, the sea was calm, its waves moving on the beach peacefully, carrying with it the white sand from the sea bottom to spread on the beach.

As Mark walked towards the sea, he bent to touch its waves. The waves were like a tiny kitten that loved to be pampered by the hands of its owner.

After long while staring into the sea, Mark said, "My body's dust would embrace your waves on the shore and would always welcome them. And my body would unite with your blue colour in the real world and eternally."

Then he stood and walked to his painting, which was still on his easel. He looked at it, and at once, his eyes filled with tears.

Then he ran toward the sea, crying, holding the tubes of the green, purple, and blue paint while his body slowly moved further into the sea.

"I implore you, with my last wish, to blend my soul with those colours and put it in her eyes. I cannot live without being with it," Mark smiled as he said his last words. *I would be part of it forever."*

The sea gave his consent. Its water covered the artist and drew him down to the seabed, doing as it promised.

So, the artist went from reality to live in his dream forever, the artist and his painting becoming one.

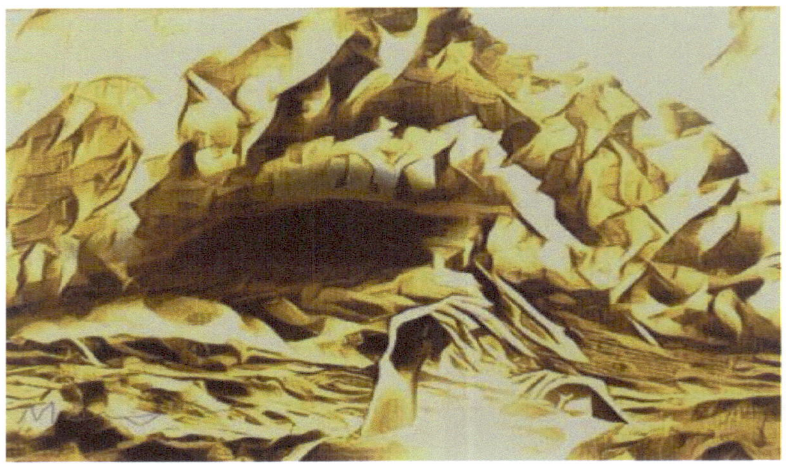

# The Orpaned Artist
## and
## the Mermaid's Eyes

Story and Paintings By
M. S David